Even Shorter
Stories V

The last of a five-book series

RODNEY PAUL WILLIAMS

authorHOUSE®

AuthorHouse™
1663 Liberty Drive
Bloomington, IN 47403
www.authorhouse.com
Phone: 833-262-8899

Published by AuthorHouse 11/08/2022

ISBN: 978-1-6655-7570-6 (sc)
ISBN: 978-1-6655-7569-0 (e)

Library of Congress Control Number: 2022921003

Print information available on the last page.

CONTENTS

NEXT COUNTRY MUSIC HALL OF FAMER

She is now as she was born a true cross breed. That beautifully full or orange crown of hair is natural as her thirty five double d's. How that came to be genetically has probably never been achieved before her. Her country western superstar dad is a natural blonde. Her super star television mom is a natural red head. She was born the true mix. Not one dominant. Orange

Her full head of hair. And before you deviants out there try to guess only her personal hair dresser knows for sure. The announcer who is her manager was referring to her husband as her hairdresser. He continued. That being announced her she is Dolly Loretta Macintre!!

The lights dimmed as her husband's Tobey cash Wayland Jennings banjo blew the roof off the sucker.

His accompanying band demolished the walls. The crowd went crazy stomping feet, clapping palms thunderously accompanied yehaws, wistles and huge bring it ons.

This stadiums inaugural openings four hundred nine thousand seats only had one empty seat and he was being detained saving the planet. The deafening a plomb would made thunder seem a mealy wimper.

Not a sound as the lights went black except for the spot light of praising blue showed she had been on stage all the while with the band. Rosin bow floor pointed, old banjo in the other she cursed and opened the melodic huge longs.

For a moment only her first notes got through. Then the bringing down the house ripping up the carpet and marbles flooring screaming applause and vocal accolades drowned her out.

Maclintire's show went the entire gambit roasing opening songs. Followed with traveling vacation from first class cruisering to hobo trains. From hitch hiking and avoiding perversions too longing for lost opportunities to great one night stands. Ending in family reunion at the Grands Ole Opree!!! The love sonnet was the shortest only four numbers.

She closes with the way she opened in darkness and the only difference is as she mentioned the names of her country hall of fame members which the entire band was the rest of the band played while the introduced member stage lefted or stage righted on his or her departure. The last on to leave did two banjo solos it was her.

No encores. The show was an hour, eleven more numbers than agreed on. Oh and the celestial cheers, roars, shouls and seemingly endless palms coming together.

CALL TO DUTY

The solar floor hit earth with damages untold in our lifetime. The emir called in all of his civilian help. All boy scouts, eagles, cub scouts, girl scouts and brownies were ordered to help. All came and all did their sworn to duty. That is all but one Cub Scout. He had stopped in for prayer before the flair hit. The priest walked, walked in as her was done giving glory.

He could not report to duty as his sore butt kept him from pulling the thirteen inches imbedded deep in this throat and run away. It was now row.

LIER OF THE YEAR

The laurels of a one million dollar emolument goes to Brian Keitt and with his payment goes this silver and white jade two fort winners' cup.

Soothing thee asemblage's inquiry, the master of ceremony fed their need to know.

A the winning reply of mister keitt was I told my wife I was late because I was having a go with my bit on the side in a three way, me, your mom and your childhood next door neighbor".

No way you live to tell that if I was yours. You aint even gon take a step toward the door.

The MC went on. The question was what was the biggest lie, you ever got away with Keitt won because he is a devout single.

When the show was about to end Keitt took off all of her clothes.

CLASS PRESIDENT

Slowly with care the opening of that window was beginning, you have heard of it I'll wager it opens when the door gets closed his fingertips caressed the chalked mathematical problem on the blackboard.

Early yesterday morning. William Henry Carbsy the driver of the Thomas Edison Middle school bus had waited an extra five minutes for Dane Kosetti he had to pull off it was winter and other stops only two but children were waiting in snow boots likely getting ready to stamp their little tooties so he put it gear and almost left. Dana's whistle blew and blew.

Carbsy never heard it. One last look in his driver's side rear view was what Dana needed. Less than a minute later she was seated next to her exact except for a gender and bloodline educational twin. Both were all a students and neither had been hate for school on a day absent in three years.

Memories

Tell me is it true that the reason you found the Yetty family because of the Himalaya's global warming? So was it getting to hot in those once frozen mountains to sustain the Yetti's normally cold atmospheric climatized conditions.

The questions themselves lended one difficulty should she answers. Her answer was a procedure from her childhood. When a trapping inquiry was enlisted of her mother towards her super genius father. He kept the answer to himself and working staff members. Certified classic.

That question can be answered easily. Should I answer now the reply I give you will make no sense to any of you? That is unless a few other questions are asked of me first. The explanation of them will clarify what the investigation for there was no legible name from the distance she stood from Carl, the investigators name tag. Getting her lead in he gave her the information she lacked INS. But while she was evading the subject, skillfully as it turned out she had wiped her sunglasses and touched the tip of her left breast jacket pocket. The signal had been given to her assistant.

Myesha Hornee approached the orators right ear lobe and fained wording.

Her startled frightened look towards Hornee was rehearsed. The two immediately left. Only inquiries and perplexed expressions remained on the news investigators as they separated.

ALL DUE RESPECT

The offspring stronger, more vicious, more deadly and with evil powers for greater than their ancestors and now there are more than one

During the year before the appearances of these so called hellspawns a new drug with the likelihood of causing hundreds of investors to profit in the billions for each investing in the soon to hit the pharmacy's the likely hood of thousands of deaths was found and re-researched. The clause in his contract legally kept him from blowing the whistle on any information on the product. He gave such notice to the executives in charge. Naturally their lawyers reminder him of non- disclosure verses his bankruptcy and a long accompanying jail cell.

His solution was except his full severance. Galiseious, his four year old girl gave him his way to a somewhat clear conscious, his freedom and his to small fortune. I would tell the newspapers daddy. His worry soon subsided. I would not tell them the product name or the company name, so you keep your word and smart people will check where you worked.

He began to wonder how soon will she be able to figure a way to hide a boy from him.

He did the fatherly thing. Hugged, squeezed kissed and told how he loves her. Then he slipped Zeba, his wife. Does Gal have a boyfriend? Seriously quizzick looking.

A moment of two of her thinking worried him. Even in her mind some doubt as to weather she has or has not also gave the little girls mother cause to pause. I don't think so.

EVER WATCHFUL

When her uncle was told his favorite six year old niece O'hare was going to have an overnight with some of the girls in her second grade. Class from school by his brother Chile, he excused himself and ran up the extra wide winded stairs to his nieces bovdoir.

Rapid tap, tap, tap, tap, tap, tap until the arrival of her consenting cook in. before the door opened her mind not only completed seated on the knowledge of whom it was that was tapping, she also was acclaimed to his caring for her solving she figured why his vast number asking entry. He knows!

Deciding to have a little fun with her much loved agnate, she wanted with no awkward interruption in his demeanor he went straight to the task at hand.

As normal the vocabulary he exspessed ten year old child, his niece was only six and carries an adult college grade student vocabulary mentality.

So went the important advice of the birds and the birds. Her hypology being the proved, she went to work on him.

His arm firmly trapped at the elbow crooked was tenderly secured both her wrist and his bicep looked in place by O'hare's tender loving head lean she closed the trap. Her ribs aching to bust out with the laughter she held inside came the verbal chiding.

Uhn, unh Chavea. When mommy first birthed me, as soon as ear lobes were in the air mi papito. carinosa mente dice a mi group young girl lesbian is the absolute best.

Chile walked down the spiral stairs to a wait family fam club. His brother and his cunada grat is had unhidable. I told you so smiles accompanying nothing gets pass us sirks. He absolutely relieved on that subject

THE SUCCESS OF THE
KHAN AND KHATUN

Before the aliens had died their machines in large numbers had gone the our water. Those water over the years saturated into the earth. Quickly deteriorating coffins and corpses unfound even in the back of some peoples yards rose, walked and devoured only living human beings.

This is the unabated, the only true and also the future cause of the living dead.

Istanbul, Turkey the only land producing edible food of any kind. Her fresh water is in abundance. Both will last almost two hundred years, as long as only six to seven people make use of them.

The main government The Turkey cumhuriyet. Hukumeti abating rictousness did not make the dire situation generally known. The TCH also knew the present population was oven ten thousand.

The entirety of the planet save for Turkey has no living beings.

On this day a thief has broken into the Sutan Kahn's bath house seeking of all things royal seals and royal letter headed paper and envelopes. Being so steathful he overhears the latest chapter of the plan to rid Istanbul of more of its population and the dictates on how much more food will be saved by the unnoticed deaths of the next seventy two to be put to death and the cause of their soon to occur demise. His family is not on the list or condemned names.

The nieces Belsp and Aosenthen had a social gathering of debutants. Lovely little ones all. The delectable enjoyed most were the candied truffles glazed in baked honey.

The attendants along with the nieces were so politically precious the palace Erdogan was tripled. He now had no way of escaping.

His hours long wait proved his incapability to avert his peaceful resting. While hidden and with a very mild snore he rested in peace. The guard discovered him so never again did he attain consciousness.

Planned and implemented a couple years ago the superior military advisor requested planes and jets be sent out the country to server the dead.

Mankind had been eaten off over a decade past. Over the years discovery enlightened the Turks that without live people to consume the walking dead were starving to nothingness. The problem was eradicating itself. Another twenty to thirty years of survival and the dead goings about would beno more.

The problem of enough food and water was the Khan's only plague, and it too was being nicely dealt with. Not being found by the dead in the mean time seemed a small problem.

The khatun feated on more than food after her nieces successful gatheral.

I Love my Mom too!

Dad why did you do this to me? You put me inside the belly of a women whose first burn is a coward. How was I supposed to look up to. I do not even know what to call him. You must know I could not bring myself to allow that type a male as is myself. No matter what happened to me in life a guy should never run home to momma after getting his how do you spell Keyster? Is Keestir even a real word? Why did leave me in a bond where that whatever it is, runs away from a guy with a knife. In front of a female having sex with that coward. To her house where she lives up the steps from the knife wielder. I was standing just up the block, so I confronted the guy after the guy got in his car. I got directly into the car window where he reached forgot and pointed his gun no more than a foot and half in front of my face. No way for me to back down. The guy pulls off. I am still alive and I ain't shot.

I was maybe eleven then. Later after a fight with a neighborhood guy almost in that spot he thinks he can give me boxing lessons!! I won that fight no matter what he would have you believe. I punched the guy up a few times with both hands. I knocked the guy on his - well he was sitting on his butt and both hands

Yeah my hand put him in that position and on purpose. Just one more thing. Thank you writer for the television and movie actor Peter Falk as Columbo. He never laid a punch, slap or push on me. I was untouched. Dad I love you this much. Thank you and mom for the skills you allowed

God to give me, but be careful where you leave yow: seed next time. OK? Love you.

ASTONISHMENT

The coresans Coalition gave her a funeral be :fitting a leader of a prominent country. First off the police inspector unmarked Townears led the procession. Then came the body of the most high class call girl in the country carried in an eight horse dawn crimson colored hearse. Followed by nine surveys from each of the countries representing the Coalition. I apologize. I just now remembered the most spectacular part of the spectacular. Five horse drawn flat conestoga wagons full of pure white colored lilies were in position after the police and proceeded. Bringing up her rear were seven more conestoga wagons load and decorated even on the wagons wheels so as only the rases could be seen. Crimson long stem roses ranging from buds to full bloosom. The horses pulling the seven wagons had only their eyes, and nostrils free of crimson tide, the ladies did my mom generously right

K.M.A.2

You just know I had to turn out to be a successful writer. The opposite side of a coin in this instance is I must be a horrible reader. Please be kind and allow my magnitudenous humility a seqway to your heart and understanding? Before being led to the world of the one who puts his thoughts to paper a fantastic reader was I scripting and paying for my words to be put to typed has denied me the worldly pleasure of meandering through someone elses mythical thoughts suddenly appearing from a non – virtual world into others viewing.

Reading has been determined non - grata tearing away at my improvement of comprehending others connotations. This is restricted to female authors. Oh so now I am supposed to dislike her printings. Meaning all hers. Not so! I do however refuse with absolute fever to set my eyes on any works from a ferns own projections. Do not I entreat the wrong yourselves via misunderstanding. The sole excuse the denial exist with me is me being male have in some vilely been infected with an unfathomed desease. I attempt to read a writing authored by a female and as try to purpose her words- a voice is attricated in cadence with letters. A female voice. So I maintain as from birth but for the brief interference of recognizing the desease my mailness by negating some I have proclivity to believe I deny myself great works.

Whomever you are singular or plural that defend me this afflication – FUCK YOU!

Brief Interlude

Just two questions about COVID -19. Question number one: compliance was supposed to be the law, sooo how did newly weds practice social distancing?

Question number two. During the COVID - 19 quarentine, how did parents ground a misbehaval offspring?

CHERRY

Doctors Senitzen Ginger Schnap and Ipple Undcherri Pi came up with the idea the vaccine that is soon to be developed to inoculate children ages five years to eleven years by mouth and by needle. Both methods the two now world renkown physicians should be developed with the memory that these vaccines are for little ones, so give them a pleasant memory. Thus both violators of the pandemic causing virus are to be engineered to for a couple of hours ensuing their treatment a child pleasing taste should linger, ice cream flavor, banana pudding flavor, a spearmint gum flavor perhaps. Let us develop it and decide on the flavors quickly.

Leave it to the hate mongers to destroy a brilliant idea. The flavor of banana over night even before the innoculations development came to a question of being racist.

SHE ASKED

The answer was right in front of me all the time. Until just now I had not been allowed to see. It has been with me over thirty years. The answer why everyone that gets close to me has miserable fortune. Just crossing one another paths here and there and lives goes on. Easy does it. Get to know me. This cut with me. Try to because my friend and year existence becomes a living hell. As if as seem as life became bearable for me ending my object loneliness brings on the head on the solar systems center and their lives go spinning down into a fuey inferno.

Yeah! I just the reason for it all. I found it out in a most precaution way. It is starring at me right now. I am unwilling to look upon it. So damned difficult not to comply to its usage. Who should I turn away from her reason. And those folk really mean anything to me. My life can go on without them easily. Only obtain is there are no obstacles that way. So damned lonely.

Walking away I find is no answer. Confrontation? Maybe. What if I become the loser. What if in the end my own life goes through hell? Confrontation!

Yeah! What if I whaa! End? Through hell? Damned? Staring me in the face? How could any of that not be? All I had been doing was looking into a mirror. How could those things have cropped up? let me get it right. Get it in order. I unlocked the door came in looked the door next my baseball cap. On the wall peg where its supposed to go. The flower I was supposed to put on Minnies coffin. I threw it into the fue place. I did not leave it at the grove site, it was as if she from her grove did refuse to accept my flowers. I can understand that though. I caused her to die. Grabbed a cold point of milk from the frog.

Took one of those chocolate chip cookies given to me yesterday from the L.Ron Hobbard book store. One bite was like eating a Cadbury candy bar. Pleased with that flavor I was about to take a goodly cold sip when, the face looking back at me from the kitchen mirror was the deepest red. Almost black like blood in an open aired moonlight setting. There were small protrusions horns at the top on either side of the front of my pate. That grin. I will never forget that grin as long as I live. It was me grinning at me. That thin blonde vee, pussy shaped mustache on my chin.

That is when the occurance it widend my eyes. I began to see the spiraling skinny serpentine like tale with a touch of boiling flame at its tip. Then with quickness of an eye blink circles of it wrapped around my neck. I fully awake! It was still there that mirror image. My left arm went backwards the pint still in my hand. The mirror was spared. With my teeth clenching, my jaw bones hardening and my glower on my mouth inffening to rigidity I with ease chose to walk away. So that is how my day went. How did yours?

THE MESSAGE PART 1

The word was given to him as an eight year old child. It was granted them. Go forth ruin his life. The forcer quickly were revilied. The soldier must be stymied now. He must not be unhindered. His growth had to be diluted. First a prominent ventured boldly yet with stealth to his knowledge opposed his gift of foresight.

Deacquistioning his foresight was easily accessed and elimination of his psychio third eye fell next with detestment. Remove from him concern and also take away his capability to maintain the loyalty of the opposite sex. His championing side raised an eyebrow as if to protest without a word less the client be seen as a weakling. His opposers request legitimated. In his enlightenings he is to be ignored. No challenge came forth, so a further illucidation was added and mocked in his rightness. And lastly impoverished.

He stood there silent. Knowing his prior would count on him having the inner fortitude to forego the few handicaps placed on him and believing success would still be accomplished, he remained so. He words would do him no positive exspanse.

As the time of departure approached leave to verbalize was given.

His first words. You wound me. Why? You place me in a world surrounded by mishegottens. Humanity is all but a totality of lost cause. The rulers of our cause you send me to are in troth fictionalizers. Should they have been deigned wild beast, their heards would stamped in injustice and evil. Most of the while prevaricating in their minds and hearts proclaiming mighteousness with their tounges. Irony in itself that the truth is spoken by them.

That same truth gives millions of followers, fame and fortune. Those followers though less afflorent are the spitted in ages. Spitted as are they.

You send me to be afflicted inflicted! You send me to the garrison of Louie who will show me hate, inflict me with bodily injuries, go against the right way send me with while you urge them on hoping me to hell to be Gehanna tormented. Yet it is me you send to save them. My place is glory is reserved. You send me to fail. My spirit and my sould shall prevail. You simple little test will I pass with effortlessness? No. pass I shall.

Without any warning he is put into an embryo. He gestates. He is born. He is here. Over the he looks up smiles, says hello to the Christ, teases Joseph, sends Mary a kiss to her creamy cheek, congratulates the soldiers of the lord, higher than that all that together, he prays to and praises jealous, he wins.

TIME MACHINE

The machine will get three trial runs. Three trial runs only. Dictated Kras Hojon. My opinion on weather the runs are a success and picked up by me and my associates is all there is. Understood me, I say yes. I say no. when will you be ready? We are ready right now. While you stand right in that spot Ms. Jeanne Bellows will take the trip. You will choose the year, month, date and time of day or night. We will send her there for one minute and one minute only.

In that minute she will have to retrieve a small non significant piece from that time and present on here return right here. One minute only so choose your time and if you have exact knowledge the piece of that period you choose to acknowledge as proof of her trip.

Hojon took a hour to figure what was a true test. One whose evidence he himself could atleast to as an actuality. His major field of study was Nazism. He knew they would know that, so that era he chose to hold back. The date and time and place? Lingered and inside he smiled. Helga one of his favorite closeknit assistants was in the oversize and overstuff lounge chair. Her opinion to that would be it feels luxurious.

This time yesterday came Hojon. Then he said aloud so all could here. My Fleetwood Cadillac Executive Lounge and I want the gift I had gave great thought to award Mrs. Leget with.

It took two minutes to prepare the machine, sent back for only one minute and two seconds for Ms. Belkas return.

This was an absolute success. Hojon had not given away the gift. Ms. Bellows put it in his hand. A platinum and two and one half carat pin in a dragons shape. It was the genuine gift.

Anyone could have surmised the pin only minutes had been where it now was not on Helga's satin Collie blazer, so he awarded it to her then and there with explanations, because she had now no knowledge of the award that as of this date had not been given to her yesterday.

Smiles and positive acknowledgements all around.

He had filled in the blanks himself about the pin. That included the half million dollar bonus given to his yesterday because the pin had not turned up and had vanished from his winter coat pocket. It was the perfect hiding place for the trinket.

The next trips request had to done incognito to the inhabitants of the time he would be sent.

The meeting was in Washington, DC. The invited attendants were wives of the Asian hand thee Asian crime organization and wives of the Sicilian clan.

This trip physical proof he did not need, he wanted proof he could accept verbally Ngyen Phon was his own man. He was called upon for times like this when one being needed non-disclosure. Ngyen was the highes paid ninja in the world. He had no scruples. Needless say lie he brought back the info. The wives had met to improve sales of their sweet snacks business planetwide. He also did not disclose the how those deadly businesslike wives planned to seize the total of the industry.

He had remembered his multi - billion are sister Moi had at time attended a similar meeting in Gnome Alaska. She he now knew is a member of the feminine hand. The womens involvement in organizing was absolutely above the knowledge of every government espionage agency. His heart for the only time in his life knew fear.

The third trip he took very personally. Upon getting back to his Tahit. Most upscale resort, he owned nine, he made calls, we will invest.

Over his mantle was a painting thousands of years old. (I say this to you as the writer of this book. Please pay adroit attention.) the images were three men Peter, John and Jesus. Jesus had on he jean prototype automatic brightness adjustable sunglasses.

LOCATION, LOCATION, LOCATION

He somewhat awake. The texture of her soaked feet and the fragrance of the potpourri from her best friend Leona's flower garden softened his demeanor and he began to look forward to the moving pictures to follow his welcomed oncoming slumber.

As he began to delve again towards pem a few threads gave way. Her pedicured large toenit ground and filed to an almost razor sharp point split his left nostril from its inside. The wet gush would have been a pleasant comfort had it not been for it being a needed lifeforce leaving.

A southerner may have allotted it a feeling of summertime mud tweenxt their toes.

Adults Only

Reiders fourteen buckaneers eleven. That was not the answer he was expecting. That was crazy he thought. That craziness just last him a half million pounds and a full holiday weekend of his wife being dugged out by Benheist Rogby team. The funds he owes is over seventy thousand short. Therefore the next four day weekend his emma would be whored out to every player doing anything and everything the fifteen men and their coaches. His gut began to somersault. He may have felt even worse had he been privy to a small bot of information. His devoted loving emma had already spalyed her wares for half of the professionals at her leisure. Willingly and loving it.

His ignorance was the ondoing of the team getting into the leagues playoffs for the Bledisole cup. As the teams plane was on landing approach a hand held soviet rocket launcher left none alive.

LOCATION, LOCATION, LOCATION II

Watching the publicized television news broadcast got her interested in the story of the private space shuttle going higher in the atmosphere than the orbiting space shuttle.

The mind could not cease to troubled without the askance of a soul question. If they build a ladder long enough from their apex, who will they meet. Pondering but a moment or few the thought of being crazy crept right on in.

You comprehend. The old adage. You are crazy if you answer your own question.

No matter which way they built the ladder, in twelve hours the other way would be interloped.

That recognition gone by – aahh. Crazy does not live here, because the twelve hour change of destination does apply on earth. Those chosen to go where few have gone before are not building the ladder to who knows where will not start the process while earthbond.

A phone call to the NASA should prove helpful. Though with today's ?#ER!," technology. To you this is inquiry is invested. What is the technical term for recorded artificial intelligence no matter what it ask of you your answer is misunderstood and you continually have to push the numver two on your telephone key pad?

If asked the answer some may give is :x:!!""??,

HOMICIDE

Numerous times it has been publicized. The perpetrator breaks down in cross examination. I didn't mean to. It was an accident. It wasn't meant to happen. First off have you ever noticed in all of those type situations that the killer always uses consonents? En you may think.

They get charged for manslaughter or murder. Try this one on for size. ELE's are extinction life events.

Your wife gets furious with you. She found out about you and her sister. She confronts you. Its true. She decides to hit you. You know the hit is coming. You prepare to duck the slap. You decide not to duck. After all you are wrong. You deserve it. she delivers the blow, only it is not a slap but a full force round house punch. It lands flush. Your head is jerked hard and backwards. A golf ball sized meteor it crashes through your head. Should she had not punched you the meteorite misses you be a foot and two inches.

She has seen plenty cup inches and feels free she keeps her mouth shut about the punch. The life insurance money is hers you cheating sob. She is easy going when giving the statement to the police officer whom arrives alongside the ambulance.

She pisses herself when the detective assigned to investigate the case is Lieutenant Frank Columbo.

How's your memory? Hint. Third paragraph, second line.

CANDY WARS

Sitting there on the veranda little Petcha his youngest eating that she had just been given of her mother before she was shewed enlighten her daddy's morning.

Catching sight of her sweet his smile appeared. He had been noticing the last three months a huge diversified plathora of people were devouring the sweet rice bills manufactured by Y.Gotta have the or rather one of the subsidiary company's owned by his little sister.

He had denied himself the case of checking the exchange not wanting to possibly allow others of the organized criminals attack on holiday confections.

Halloween fell first. Razors, pills and poisons found in the little gifts shortened the number of children trick or treating almost ninety five percent.

The non – discreations of females killed saint valentines day celebrations. To further cause the quitting of chocolates given the criminal caesarettes enlisted the employment of one mister Rodney Paul banks wallace Williams to come up with an idea to help remind the men what their uh, uh – better halves liad done with others while their men backs were turned. Almost every female cheated on their boyfriends, significant others, betrothed and husbands.

The idea the women accepted showed how devious the women minds were and still are actually the is not more so.

Rodney gave a slight mental nudge that VD day no not venereal disease day but valentines day could still be altitudeness. Easily but you're here – heee – hee woman a four piece sampler, one rose and an inexpensive bottle. Then go on up by buying your daughter (s) a twenty pound box expensive chocolates, the dozen long stem roses and a valentine's card two feet high and eight feet long.

It went over huge with the caesarettes.

Those brains knew the new - do - wells inside out. They knew their feminine sisters well enough too. The woman loved the VD idea. All the held onto was the idea that their daughter's sweet stash would be raided by themselves with ease. The idiots! Thought the criminal heads of the world and rightly so the Handie and cosanustrettes knew those male dead beats wouldn't ascend the daughters of their own bloodline as little queens, little princesses. Most wouldn't even take the time to visti their own child. Again the venomous brains were correct.

Saint valentine's day died.

KATHY IN THE BOUDOIR

Had it not been for his pride those tools women call toys would not have been replaced. A smarted man may have left them where they were. She bought newer ones, more modem ones. He figured at her funeral in his demention she must have been faithful as far as human extra relations went. If he had only knew.

Back to the subject the newer ones were longer some supple. The one she that her life had almost penetrated he asophgust at the point of her lungs top. The esophogial slime eased it down as it was a straight trip when lying on her thoracic and head titled towards the floor. Putting it in the back was a story of another color. Even with the lubricant the maneuvering of the smaller intestine did not go so well. She was loving the escrutiating blissful pain. Her perforated lower small circuslike balloon tubing was perforated. Over time it patty duked her.

You Didn't Watch

The alien gave the Department of Defense's chief Igles matise white a full months notice by united states postal service letter mailed directly to his office and a must be signed for designation. The help this planet was being offered it did not get a chance to enlist. The letter so thoroughly sent to lend earth and was given no merit It was ignored. Then the film was shown on the television station who paid for videos made of the football game by two spectators who caught some of it on a cellphone and a mother filming her son. The boys dad was serving his country overseas.

Perhaps she caught the couple of the now infamous super child because of her slight embarassment. Every time she took her time to film her buy he was the second string half back sitting on sidelines.

Never the less every tube news had the movies of supernatural plays done by a fourteen year old child. And as you now have it the chief of the DOD found out about it from his ten years old gran daughter. A phenom in her own right too. She stood five feet eleven and one eight of an inch skinng as a rail as the slogan gees. An outright genious who I was one hundred fifty and steadily getting higher

Her mom Gladys had triple phd's and was about to close out her four bachelorette. Her father mere educational paper had only attained two doctorates. Bolstering him needfully when standing next to his wife he also had three more bachelor degrees and nine other associates Heinn Mears was on his way to earn the couples sixth billion. He could not yet be entrusted with the tital of Hollywood baby Mogul.

Never daunting his amazing grandchild's intelligence he exuburendy cradled her wasteling excused himself of the others present and casually listening yet with full attention to her words walked minding her gate to her nine feet purposely projection on the wall in her room where she restarted the fourteen year old football leagues season opening game.

As her grandfather it was and is still his duty to check his children's and his great grand children's health, totally. He never slouched on his duty since first becoming a father seventy one years and one month past.

The game ended three days ago.

Powerful Men in Fear

The major players had arranged the peace treaty to shut down the threat of the newly formed. Scandinavian Cartel. The feast included steaks two inches thick. Baked and braised musaka Portibellos. Steamed asparagus extremely tender and not slimey. Broiled red beets and white reddish in a sauce that could make an extremely religious Rabbi sin. There were a plathora of other dishes but I think you have an idea.

The mayors, governors and US senators of the conjoined eleven states all attended. The expected problem was going to occur in that large of a capacity.

One of the Asian top criminal empire boss picked up two empty platter trays that were about the be adorned with food that would have made King Solomon blush with envy. He did just that himself but with different types of deliciousness

Some of the others noticed and anger was building up inside them when he made a move that stilled their anger completely. He took outside the highly reported event, but highly report from the outside and gave to a group of homeless vagabonds along with thirty plate and plenty silvery colored plastic utensils. When a couple others saw his intent then in turn attained napkins and few empty large litter bags with the warning to the needy leave no refuse on the premises. Do not give those people a reason, emphasing reason, to look down on you. Out came small bottles of imported champagne and a few cases of beer from Germany.

The meeting closed out after after the reported time. The politician were told to call their respective headquarters to deviate all anxiety. Remember most politicians are also, political enemies of one another. If you are still doubting, than remember the Kennedy's and George Wallace along with his Ilk.

A LETTER IN THE U.S.A.

He stepped away from the field when the game was over. The team he had played in the first half for was leading at the half by seventeen points. He refused to play in the second half. He was waiting on the sidelines hoping for a visit from the Secret service, maybe the Federal bureau of Investigation. He wanted for a meeting that none of the above attended.

The team he had put up front in the first half of the game had lost it without him. His team members, coached manger and fans leered when they did cast their eyes on him

When he got outside the football field's fences his uniforms and the accessories accompanying it fell to the ground. As a few times during the game only with him fully attired he disappeared. Look up in the sky. If you could see a naked child ten miles above on a sunny clear blue sky the fourteen year old reappeared and flew away.

When he did fly he flew fast, so fast Branson's unity twenty two did not notice as he passed it. He flew so fast that no rador on earth picked him up. he flew so fast that no interstellar satellite even noticed him. In hasty departure his disappointment in the US political power dismayed him so much that neither he nor any of his race would ever again be seen by human kind.

Candy Wars Concluded

Santa clause is all but out of business. Mrs. Clause is now a heroine and crack addict. She is all skin and bone from a steady diet of over a million different men's semen.

Those who have indulged in her yet wont even buy toys because of the news being spread around the little spinning blue marble. Christmas is dead. Candy canes are only being sold at a four for one discount after Christmas.

Valentines day as Christmas we all know is dead. We see it in the streets. One balloon filled with helium where there used to be ten twenty. The candy sales are down by ninety percent.

Halloween shot to shit. And in doing so, we kept our own little tit suckers cut of harms way, even from the nineteen sixties when we had a some little bigger tit suckers bogart away their trick or treaty booty. No candy to take home. No reason to go out to get it.

Allowing their easter rabbit and baby chick pets to die was as brilliant an idea as the idea the first girl Gladys had to make fire. Halloweens celebration has gone into the fire of Gehenna.

We have won and our snacks are in every store from nastiest, dirtiest favela to our own humbly occasionally visited delicacy emporiums.

Success tastes, smells and feels upstanding. Congratulations to us all. Our business being done as a conglamorate, I make the motion we as of tomorrow at eight o'clock 2020 go back to our cut throating each other ways/

Second that is heard by numerous votes. The meeting is adjourned. Furthermore I am one guy who is not going to miss the insult of giving away candy on whatever on my own birthday

The woman was in her seventh month. Already twins had been determined. One boy one girl. As in most pregnancies if not all pregnancies the inside of her belly goes about the actions most if not embryos do shortly prior to their exiting their ensentenced imprisonment. That is the most likely reason for the unruliness. They have come to the realization that their rights to freedom are being violated. Yet we so called educated people never put a stephoscope up the chanel to insure them the process of their freedom is shortly at hand and give apologies for their unjust imprisonment.

The mother is punished for not understanding. This but not in full and it is just to wish no saddle blocker have been given her. With male and female twins the girl understands this though later in life

Prison Awareness's

The boy only has an idea of it should he be there as an adult when his own tiny one comes mentally laughing into the world. We hear him crying and do not comprehend the only reason for the tears in he has not mastered laughing yet. Nor do we remember our birth that we cried only because we were angry that we could not laugh at our parents as does our newborn.

Then the noise stops. You see we have also not comprehended that the female newborn stops crying when she finally realizes that water slide ride was scary but fun. She has yet to consume the premonition she has had that one day she will be that ride. She smiles realizing she is going to give her future daughter such glee.

I keep figuring the female parent may have a glimpse of the future day and holds back some of the if you only knew.

This is where if I was the father get even more confused. All I have been able to notice is the dirty names the woman I love has stopped shrieking in the air at me and the infants crying has elapsed when that tiny mouth goes on that nipple.

Since I really haven't seen one crying as the nipple goes in only the imagination of the gleeful wabling stops as that bumpy bud enters the newborn's mouth. Those things are magical.

However I am the sort of dad that when the dual genders are born I look both into their eyes. I listen intently to both of their heartbeat rhythms and inquire did they both behave while imprisoned?

I have to take of you me leave. The children's warden is calling me.

Did I tell you the part that when the boy was born that he grabbed hold of Ms. Marishka's the nurse titty.

I remember not to be to wide eyed. My warden was looking right into my face.

There is a smirk on me face as I go the twins are at their grandparents.

FRANCE'S LETTER TO YOU

DNA right good idea. Now who did she say your dad is?

Count yourself lucky. Even though most people in this country do not know that on that sper of time she had a thought on your dad. The reply came in a neg. she lied to me. That is all I care about. Giving a positive hope come via a neg. I said. There is still a goodly plan for accertaining his identity. Not perfect mind you, but a chance exist. A chance is more than my gave me. To heck with that. I said and continued. We check you DNA against the police arrest records. If he has served even three days time, at once mind, since nineteen eighty, three his DNA is registered. A match gives you your dad. It is only a shot. Take it.

You know. I continued a small idea I have could let you know why she did not tell you. But so you wont take a swing at me, listen to this. So research on the Argentinians taught me in Argentina only one fourth of the families have two parents, the other three quarters have about seventy two percent moms with kids.

Leads me to belive promiscuity there a heap of dads don't know they have a kid. If you understand what I am saying do I need to put put on my fencing helmet or are we good?

My other lead is some do not give as much as a damn about the quicky. So there goes her memory onto the next guy and mix her child. Emphasis on her. Oh one more thing. Should you have said that to me.

Hand delivered.

GONE

Misses Gross sour cream and onion potato chips lunch bars. Potts ice cream: da ja blu water: roos sneakers: brogan boots: father, mother: child: mint julips candy: are all gone.

My thesis was being prepared for things of my past. I wish to return to me. My attempts to find their makers even my mom and dad led me to find so many more items missing from what I do contemplate now that noticing them as I decend and consternation sets me as not noticing during those departures cancels my non concern in halting what is now non- oblivious. Their oblivion.

I end this now with friendship as the list is too much for my mind to handle. I think I shall just blame chucky.

THE ARMOR CAR HEIST

Focus on the task at hand. The order came from third precinet police on the street superviser corporal Rand ovuhr. The new recruit officer Idrive foor hertz took a very good survey of the otherwise unoccupied area and unhelstered his Glock nine millimeter.

I don't think we'll our weapons. At least not yet. Put your weapon back in your holster said Ovuhr to hertz with ease of mind. It is said that primary duty of a policeman is to go homesafe to his loving family when his shift for the day is over.

Providence perhaps should have gotten that message to night shift officers to return home when daylight arrives in the same safe manner supervisor Ovukr may have made it. he did not pay more attention. He was at close to total calm when patrolman hertz the advise. For if he had been attentative a moment longer then the nine millimeter piece of lead from hertz's glock would not have gone through the now at total ease head profuciously leaking Ab positive blood from both the entrance and exit holes thereof.

HIMAPHRODITE

When Johathan Witee was born the test given him revealed one secret. The doctor came quickly when given the most incredible news the fifty year practicing ObGyn had ever been told about a newborn he had delivered.

Going over the results of the blood test for a third time the exasperation set in sitting him on his thin honey narrow romp.

The broad shouldered vaginaed girl he delivered to Marvin and Mercy Macintosh's lab work proved the full vaginaed newborn had no X chromosomes. There also was no penis. Not even a dwarfed appendidge where a penis could have been stymied. Same same condition was non remarkable as to testis. The only notable sex organ was the fully developed vagina and all that completes that package.

The idea of having a stiff Tanquere before greeting the child's parents with this here to fore unfounded even un thought of before this day's rodamontand.

His only way to approach this with the progenitors was to be plain and forthright. His practice ran through his brain, Mr. and Mrs. Macintosh, Marvin marcy your child has no X chromosomes. Even with the vagina, your child is a male. A, a boy.

Overpayment

Awakening in the morning alertness slapped him in the face in the same manner as wife entering your executive office unannounced by your pants down while being adorned by the former secretary your wife had reservation about and had you dismiss her.

No questions. Answers only. I am in the port smith motel. I don't have to check I bet some of my cash is missing. I saw them go threw my wallet and out the door in the briefness of my eyes opening. Never do mescaline, windowpane, opium, hashish and Schlitz beer together again. Great couple of rimmers.

Eight years later.

You are going to win this election. It had been designed to put you exactly where you are going. These are to keep you in line once you Vice president. The negatives went into the burning fire place. The WWXXD radio investigative commentaror bid goodbye to Mrs. Loki, gave her a little hug and a peck on her right cheek as he was going to exit the door.

The female seventy years old and looking every bit of forty, forty one, or forty two, called to her son to bring Joe, the commentator, that bottle of Rye from the bar. As her son turned to retrieve the drink, his mother firmly and sexually offered her ringed hand on the peeker of Joe Orand and Orand kissed her flesh above her v shaped blouse while lying his flat palm on her flat ass.

Had he soon to be Vice-president son not been present the action would have gotten blistering and nothing restrained.

Getting into her Bentley Molsanne she looked completely out of place by the eyes of any but the wealthy discerning. Her hair dressing appointment waited. More than half the bottom of her soft white skinned buttocks in full view. Daisy duke never showed such emplage in public but she soon would. Her best friend already in the front passenger sent lovingly with some jealousy in her tone called to her, you twat. That is exactly what was showed as her first leg began to enter in order to make the usual hastey get away. The mirror side of the flap taped is a Benjaman Franklin one hundred Dollar bill. The eight year old bill still maintains its crisp newness.

The phone was handed to him. Mister Trevor Mister Vice-president. The VP excepts the phone hears eight words. Hangs up the phone and makes a call on his breast pocket cell.

This is what I need the vice -president states into his cell. A minute later, okay. I'll get it right now. His mother leaves the spa and heads towards her house. She arrives. The secumty gate is raised. The mansion her is one hundred fifty years from the gate. As her car passes the gate the nine bedroom stone structure makes a large unfathomable noise as it collapses. It explodes into flames with the whirling of the dust cloud.

From over over a mile away the house keepers tum to the area the sound has come from. after passing the mistress on the road bare moments ago horror grasps all the stareing, stiffened bodys.

Yesterday.

He has played ball thus far. Why the warning?

Tomorrow.

The job is done. Good. Now, of the job being done was a code for make the call. He did. The phone was answered. Not a word said. He waited exactly a minute and sent the code for its on. The Devinci Code move sold us a bill of goods. There is only one it in Illuminating then hung up.

Justice denied

He had stolen the idea of Amelia Gonzalez and been found shot in his head point blank range. The weapon used a ten gauge shot gun.

Amelio Gonzalez Amelia's brother had done the deed. Amelia and Pepito their little brother were the witnesses. The court case ended years afterwards. Amelia was awarded the half billion dollars and ownership of the human washing machine's patent.

No Biological Heir

He went from rags to riches with the invention most major car dealers purchased his idea from the automobile industries manufacturers.

Pure genius it was extracting the heat from a running auto, truck, bus and a train. Then forcing it out to the surface the vehicle ran of. It melted snow and ice while moving. With over a million vehicles on snowy road across the planet, and more being made and sold every year he went from riches to being wealthy. Then he broke the ceiling to the plateau of the vastly wealthy.

Obtaining the step on the ladder of one trillion dollars being any other in six years and with no children he died.

Governments where he had citizenships USA, Brazil, China and Bangladesh fought it out in a court for the division on the money and proportional ownership of his invention. Nice funeral.

You need a pillow

You are going to get this much good advice. Dismiss it if you choose. A woman is not like a man. Think what you do when you pee. What? When you pee where does your pee come out? Answer me. My urethra. Where is your urethra? Inside my penis. Keep that in mind. Now when you have sex where do you ejaculate from. My urethra. Great! Now I will clarify why I asked. When a woman pees where does she pee from? Her vagina. Right. Now when a women comes where does she come from? Her vagina. Right. The why difference is your penis can go in her vagina in two different holes. One she pees from which is near the top of her vagina and on the inside. The other near the bottom of her vagina. That is what you might call her pussy. Her pussy should you decide to call it that is not, I repeat is not where she pees from but is where she gets to become pregnant from your semen. So I tell you this advice if you want to impregnant your wife than stop! I say stop! Fucking her in her pee tube. Stupid! That was the thought in his doctors mind when the was brought up to him by his patient. He did not like this patient. So the answer to the question, why can't I get my wife pregnant? He answered I don't know.

It's True

—————◆◆◆—————

Ah man. I do not believe that virus is real. It is just a play for the pharmaceutical conglomerates to stay in business and for some of them to get richer still.

Bush babies. You do not know of what you say.

Believe me. Covid-19 is not real. If the covid virus is not serious then tell me. Answer this question. Why are so many people in hospitals? Why are so many dying? Answer that hunh!

Okay. First off that is two questions. None the less. Here is the true viable explanation. Think if your meager minuscule little brain will allow you. What you call COVID-19 never made any human being ill until the government said we have a new virus called COVID-19 and so and so and so are the symptoms of the virus. Still no deaths. The governments you need to be tested like a bolt of lightning more sicknesses and now the deaths. Now regress a second before the test only a few hypochorides were reported. None before the announcement of it remember? Let me like COVID to baseball. For a decade a players bats in the three hundreds. He steals a hundred bases a year. He does consistently earn the golden glove. His runs batted in average in one hundred one per reason. His home town is elated with. Other team home towns revere but hate him playing against them.

All of a sudden he knocks one out of the park. A home run. His only only. Now when he plays due to his record and his fame he becomes a home run threat. That is covid-19. Okay so over his next eight years nine more home runs. His other stats remain constant but the pandemic has arrived he has hit ten COVID-19's. his last at bat in his career, he is retiring, he hits a ball in the outfield so weird that with his base stealing speed he runs all the way around the diamond. That is called the vaccine. Only one player on the other team noticed something, so he asked the umpire to see the baseball. He explains to the umpire quietly why. The ump gives the opposing player the ball and second base is tagged by the foot of that player now holding the ball. The batter who ran the base missed stepping on the second base as he ran around and is called out. That is called a variant. Now the pharmaceutical company's developing the vaccine love it. We need a booster shot. Children used to got free gists at some games. That is when it was reported children could not get covid. No more free gifts. It costs too much. It cuts into the drug profits, sooo guess what no more free gifts for children. Now covid-19 needs a vaccine for them. Ah this is okay it was probably all those runny noses. Thank the good lord the sneezing could not pass on the virus. 0 we need more money. Let us blackmail the pharmaceutical people. The brains at the vaccine company's say sell masks.

I say. See you. Next pandemic.

In signing off the probable truth to this one particular conveyance stands upright in the sequence of events re- reported are out recorded sequencial order. I chose to leave it that way. Do you think a possibility exist I have obtained a soupcon of lethargy?

No could it be that that insanity is trying to creep its way to me? This is the point where I wish again that I had a mate, so I could say sweetheart please pass me that loosely rolled VnExpress. That in my mind if it were true I sing to my mate - good night sweetheart and to all others - it time to go!

BEING RIGHT

You and pearl Bailey have styles that are twins. So I ask you is your sobuviquet your pen – name Pearl Bailey? No. I only use the moniher this book is under.

Surprising. I have a book that reads of this exact style. Tremendously imaginative the two of you.

Maybe I'll run across Bailey someday and compare notes. There you are all signed.

That is why a got a copy of the list. It was in the store I saw my latest. The same one at the signing I just left. By pearl Bailey was at the covers bottom. The first word I read gave me an intense feeling of joy. Half way into the first sentence my joy emensely hopped up.

This sentence I had written three years ago. Turned out I had written the full publishing.

While looking for the ways to punish the thieves of my ideas I watched to news on television and a true or false realization came into mind. For over forty years they why had not been answered to the question. Why does a family not punish the molester of a child. Some answers were anointed with my rejection of the forthcoming answer. the molestors were uncles, aunts, stepbrothers, stepsisters in note family. Excepable rapist. No now two or more family need psychological treatments. The single mother's boyfriend?

Her excuse for not having the pedifile cuffed and shackled, she got another mate. Then a many occasions the second one did it too. The other dipey parent that got the first ones discard now has the promising unnatural fate for the next little human being in line because the fust one did not prosecute him or her.

The female parent in almost all who allowed the rapist to not go to jail if not before her child being raped than assuredly after the defiling winds up in a group situation and participates with both sexes there. The parent thinks little of having in some cases a gay treated little boy is gay herself. I feel horrible, if I could feel anything. Why did it take me so long to figure it out? Philadelphia Pennsylvania in the United States of America has gone gay. So why spare the children those experiences.

First move get in touch with the published and everyone I sent a copy of the book to. Second check to be certain the copy of the book and my handwritten one is still in my safe deposit box.

The next week when I had a break from the tour the visit was paid to TD bank center city 19103 zip code. In the vault went with me my cell phone camera and the bank's supervisor. She did as I needfully requested stood there and witnessed that I put nothing in the box but only took two hundred photos of the hand written copy the was plagiarized. She witnessed I took nothing from the vault. Step one to my law suit complete.

One week backwards. The call ended with me told nearly what I earlier envisaged. Now to decide, handle this myself or lawyer up.

Three weeks into the next year and there I stood. Short sleeve white T Shirt with full action posed Marvel's red guardian picture. White denims and white socks with white low cut new sneakers, no one recognizes me. Thank you could mask. White, I have been here almost six hours. My mind is on the Texaco Ranch hotel across the parkway. The doorman opens the door. Holds it open for an old guy with his scanty dressed arm candy. The revolving door goes around. Okay now I can cross the parkway. I step right next to but in front of him. The light goes out. I see the darkness enter both his eyes. I also see the consciousness go bye - bye. First there is a step backward. Then both his sort of hop up in the air, one not as high as the other. I have his full body in view. The hop is not high off the pavement. Only an inch or so. Then comes the second hop. All of his motions have gone backward. He hits the ground- out cold. I walk away. See you in court is my thought. Now city blocks away. I had began to jog quickly as soon as I turned the first corner I arrived at. Picking up my speed here and there as I joked and made my way may way to my car slow I pulled away. See you in court now comes to my mind. I am away and without handcuffs.

My next thought is President Trump was proved right about needing to build that wall.

Love story?

We had been together for now on near half a year. Her Pakistani home grown patois got to me under my collar at first auditory perception. Me being one refined man attended to protocol when first time acquaintance making. So even as my eyes stayed glued to her beautifully white eyeballed hazel occulars my thoughts stayed then as thought time and also right now below my collar.

Believe in this please I even then wished as I continue to purvey her underarm hairs.

Now I contend you thinking me gross. World you think me less should I say to you this has been a love sonnet to her.

Wishfully thinking.

Had she not be a misses, perhaps my code would have become pellucid.

If not. Just one more poser. My brain stands erect.

SWEET

She turned her back and he swallowed the last of the vegetable steak sandwich she had prepared for him. As unappetizing as it was to his tastebuds and solidly settled his stomach was going to turn sour at the thought of meals right then and there he accustomed his mind to accept a lifetimer of bad meals and assisting in keeping a clean home. He knew it would be the greatest move of his life and threw the years the decision proved him right.

Sixty one years later.

He stood there for seemed like hours to the adult standing there beside him. Egged to move on he did. He sat next to his mother. All of his step siblings sat on the same row as he. Ten years would go forth being he would remember that day. Only then did he comprehend that on that day he had attended the funeral of one of his greatest allies. She had passed away having more love for him then she had for any other ever her parents, her husband and her siblings. His aunt who he did not remember seeing until that day she lay in that stainless steel stain and silk decorated box her on this moment recognized as her coffin.

He did show a small but of his humanity in the moment he thought but not a full thought. He still had not matured enough to handle that type of caring yet. But the part his machinelike mental presence he did posess captured wanting when she called my name as she did came through clear very faintly.

For into his future he showed himself in a way he never showed for others. He did glimpse that he hoped that his long ago passed unt did not have in her mind he needed her forgiveness. That then he was an uncomprehending pre - juvenile but as an adult, he understands.

Now out of the vehicle he screw the eight inch sealed at both ends double steel tubes hollow in the middle to the steel for. hollow barrel. After adjusting his COVID-19 face mask he enter the corner store places two rounds directly at close range into the former human traffickers head. He does not take the time to view his art work. He leaves gets into the getaway vehicle and travels in the direction away from the camera on the wall outside of the poppy's.

THE SLETH DEMON

During the eight to nine hundred time line the sleth Demon was put into his supposedly thousand year hibernation.

Every thousand years the demon arose for torture, mam and slaughter. Depending on how it took to put it rest for the next thousand years more or fewer victims it took. The longer it was able to keep away vengeful hibernation the more victims. In the mid nine hundred men thought it put to its centuries rest. In the past the warriors putting it under always left the ritual to put it away until ten decades had past. That time a victory was achieved but it was not put to sleep for the thousand years as was thought. Unknown to men of that tie they had killed the demon.

When the nineteen hundreds arrived the demons children arose in its place.

Word of Mouth

George was talking to a long life friend. Joe, George said and further communicated to Joe. I went on vacation to Camaroon last year. I stayed at the East Jablip Hotel. Their service was par excellenc. Hmmm, sounded Joe as if to doubt maybe only to inquire of George to illucidate. George catching the murmer chose to give an example of his information. For instance George brought for to Joe, I spilled a gulp or so of my coffee on the spread on the twin sized bed. The coffee being in its liquid drinkable from had soaked into the sheets and wet the mattress cover. Immediately I had gotten off of the bed. Shortly I phone room service. I was assured by the front desk a clean spread and a clean set of linen would soon be forthcoming. Well I did not wish to cause room service to be in the room for more time than would be absolutely mandatory, so I removed the bed covering quickly I tossed them on the floor near the double white closet doors. Removing the bed coverings gave me adaquant reason to ring up the desk again. The service prisons word was given to me that the problem of the heavily urine stained mattress would be replaced within the next forty eight hours, sure as this morning came. After last night two days later a new coffee stained mattress replace the urine stained one. Uhh, I thick the stains were coffee

The two grown men realised at that moment that four year old J0 Beth, Joes daughter, the middle one of his three was in the den listening with somuch intent. Her father snuggled her and baid her say hello to his buddy. She with the grace of high breeding compiled. His mister George. I hope you are well. I am feeling great George replied. The two men knew each other so well they both families had photos of both set of children when babies asleep in the playpens. With genuine smiles on all the faces

Joe patted his four years olds bottom kissed the top of her afroed head and led him towards the living room where her resting mother was sipping tea with but a drop of cognac. Jo Beth looked her mother directly in her eyes

Finally confident the eyes of her matriarch rested completely in her own Jo Beth said to her mother and said mommy mister George is teaching daddy how to use profanity

This even shorter story is dedicated to Doctor William Henry Cesby whose stories of children have enthrated me for almost a little bit more than, fifty years. Oh one more thing. About admitting what you did admit, I pray Mrs. Camille doesn't kill you. To my reading followers, if ever my wife walks in one me with as naked woman and I in the oct, I am the student of Saturday night Live. Google it.

UNFAITHFULNESS

Jacob at the party went out to the veranda his wife closely trailing him. She stood beside him. Whap!! He face stung. That was for not telling me that I came home with a venereal deseasen he said.

The two of them went back inside rejoining the get together.

The Vigilante Principle is Illegal

We'll get them even if we have to get one at a time. When we're in position we hit you up on your jack. Keep it on vibrate. If none of those three bitches are there pull it out your pocket and answer. answer before six rings. That's important, if one or all of them are there don't answer. well make our move. To make sure we get at least one of them when they see get out the short they gone haul ass. You be in last place so they don't see you pop one. With us chasing and blasting you shouldn't be seen. That way you can still hang out. I hope we get all three. We get set starting tonight.

One of the three died that night in the well planned attack. The city camera on the corner caught the beginning of the attack. It did not see the plant shoot one of the hoods that were in the group. When they fled all ten of them got out of the camera's viewing range. A second of the targets took a hit in the right side.

He lived, for the night. Two days later in Can Guaorra's hospital he succumbed. Only one more child rapist left on the list

As the crowd of thugs were chased away from where they had been gathered two had shots rang out. One the first shot hit the side of that one who would die in the hospital. The second was to be for the third target had she been there. Both ordered to shoot wild one slug as to not let the plan be fully found.

No arrest were made. No clues to the assailants identity were ever found. Those two killings had brought the city's homicide total to over five hundred that year and Christmas was still to come.

Sometimes the legal authorities cannot do the work or some part of the job taxes pay them to do, mainly due to parental inadeguacy. Thee inadeguacy being certain crimes single women refuse to report. This is an alternatives

TESTIMONY

It has been taught to us children and our parents that according to the Holy Bible that sin entered the world through one man. They do go on stating that man was Adam of the book of Genesis while in the Garden of Eden.

In my now aged state my mind leads me to the belief that what I was taught on the subject of the world's first sin has to been taught to me incorrectly

Adam knew not to eat of that forbidden trees growings by word of god himself. Eve knew not to eat of it by means of being Adam's rib. When your brain is told something your rib gets the news. Some would caution here to validate the foresaid. I say to them raise your arm. Could you have raised your arm without your brain giving the message to do so? Some push further in today's electronic stimulus thesis. Again they are now aware at the speed that electronic signal is sent to the brain and returned along with the order from the brain.

Guess what knowledge female had to be stimulated to eat of the tree. Did you guess it right? Yes you did or no the answer is Satan. Without such a stimulus, Eve had never even thought to disobey. This I think the first sin entered the world through an angel.

It was written that God evicted the two from the garden but before God did God slew an animal to clothe them as eating what the agreement was not to eat made the couple aware that they were naked. Which reminds me just whom outside of the garden was going to see them? Go figure.

To the point of which I plan on making most optical to you. It is written God slew an animal and clothed the two, Adam and Eve. Here again god agreed to clothe them. Why? Again go figure.

The point is an Hawking is and this includes me, a picture Adam and Eve upon being evicted has the appearance of Barney and Betty Robbie in their article or the look or core people in paintings. What if we are wrong.

God is benevulent, so now I picture Adam in a four piece attire long trousers button down shirt, vest and hat added to cowboy boots.

Eve went out of the garden with Adam in a leather thong with matching bra two sizes too small accessorized with leather high heeled knee high boots. And on her crowning glory a long billed baseball cap.

LITTLE CHARLES PENSKY

Little Charles Pensky felt left out. He wanted to go up to the front of her classroom and confront MRs. Belt his psychology teacher. He had raised his hand. He was given her sign to put it down. That look of hers peering over the top of her eyeglasses along with the arm Bent at the elbow and her pointer finger poked towards the ceiling left no doubt of her intention on not being disturbed at the moment meant not right now.

She went over every student in the classes test scores one by one. Not his. He patiently wanted knowing he did well on the exam. He never scored under a ninety on those ones where the top score was one hundred.

This week nobody's came below a seventy eight. The test was not an easy one. She was one hell of a teacher.

The class ended and Charles went up to her desk. I was expecting you she said to him. I know what you are going to ask me about. You did not get your test returned to you. Charles she went on to say he force any reply came from her student. I am going to ask you just one question and how you answer it depends on the grade you get for the test.

I turned in my test Charles affirmed to her and in the same sentence questioned her right and reason for this intrusion on his work.

I know she replied. Your question you get was missed on all but two other students turning. Get it right and you earn a one hundred. His answer to the question was Beovier and it was precisely right. He knew he was right without her telling him.

Before he left the classroom he just had to ask in his youthful exhuberance can I have my paper test now? She answered him no Charles. There was a slight bit of success in her contenance. She was decided he would next ask why. Cutting the inquiry off she told him you remember Burton right? It really was a question but she negated any answer changing the askance into a statement in intent and purpose. Burton was her snow white full grown great done. She ate it.

Enelloc – Satan's Little Sister

This story begins and ends with the same line. Now let us begin along with it.

My name is pronounced A-Na- Yok. Only twenty four hours ago enelloc got the news of her only full blooded brother. He was million of years in existence before her creation. He had been at the state of most excellent in his honored order.

He fell and when he did caused sin to enter into the world. So he inadvertently or bylan of his own design (advertise alert!) may have cause the people who were to perish due to lack of knowledge to become sinful. After all when sin entered the world what would have been the big deal if there were none to be infected by it. The phrase god took Adam and put him into the garden. Could this serve to prove that God also let some he did not put in the garden of Eden? By the way did that garden belong to someone (Eden)? Was it named after someone or something named Eden. Could it be a part of a larger structure or area is there possibly some other reason?

Enelloc had all that information and so much more. Only she was unsure off how to avenge her sibling. The thought of how to change his destiny never occured to her. if it had all the damage she caused may never have happened.

With the power of suggestions as Satan she caused hurt and pain

The examination started instantly when she touched the planet. Setting the trap one Tellulah Banks. Tellulah is an eight year old girl daughter Bret Moverich and Leslie Banks.

Your daddy would care to drink a hot cocoa. Ten minutes later whipped cream topped with the chocolate mini marchemellows on my daddy the best cup of instant cocoa is placed in the hand of Bret. He took the time to stop repairing the ding in his eight cylinder VOlkswagan Attend.

The cup sat down for a kog and a smooch. There would be time for one more smooch at bedtime. After that when parents and daughter were fully asleep the spring to the trap sprung.

Your daddy needs a very hot cup of coffee. Boiling hot in was delivered. Quiet. Do not awaken him. He will not get enough sleep. Tip toe to him. Open his mouth some. Slowly now, deliver the drink. It was still bubbling.

What the demon angel did not know is her power grew vasdy every tike a second went dead to be mourned by the new arrival until it's pending death no longer pended and onwards to again a new arrival.

She had no way of knowing that her well placed indignation of torture had also gone out to every eight year girl who lived with her dad that was asleep copied Tellolahi's good and kind and painfully blistering jesture. She is not going to be a problem for long. Four cheubim went to pay her a visit. Zecks the leader of the four spoke to her. He mispronounced her name.

I refuse and the four of you cannot stop me. Again he spoke when the quartet again found Her. Again he mispronounced her while using her designation pertating to her relation.

She had been finished the constitute of the fully molly she had planned to havoc. The forest thousands of acres of them were set a blaze. So much average the fire would destroy homes, business, injure and end numerous lives for decades.

A barage of enalmities did she wreak and each and without exception the Cherbian arrived and verbally admonished her.

The last time was exactly twenty three hours after carnage intially began she let out a power when unleashed destroyed the cherubim. As they were rapidly dismantling she did pronounce my name is pronounced A-Na-Yok

WHY DIE TRYING?

Dental images in motion is what he sought. Believing in what you do is one method you can represent without reservation. Getting his message to the political heirarchy is a venue to get started to that end.

Aids, cancer, diabetes were a few the big wigs voted to put plenty of money in. When the money flowed the direction chosen was in the definite direction of pills and supplies those illness married to them.

The cost of the twenty thousand copies did not don't either of his checking account. Optimistically those few dollars spent would turn into just under or above a million dollars in his pockets

Her Rantbesa DDS chief executive officer of the world wide dental association barely hunched a shoulder when the first hundred or so mimeo graphs came to his home office but when those turned into thousands and then ten thousand he began noticing the copies came from more then three hundred countries. Each copy signed with birthdates, addresses, phone numbers.

Seventy people each copy and the full twenty thousand had not arrived so those he was yet aware of.

Lots of people cannot afford implants. If you dentist stick together world wide you can force the government of the major country to pay for them. Helo put a smile on all peoples. The undersigned back you up. So was written and sealed on the flyers. The last two words on the hand bills – WE VOTE.

An enhancer was given to every country.

One printing in every country was given an extra worded flyer requesting that the organization receiving that particular flyer print one hundred copies of it and pass the seconds to people and places for signing and forwarding to their own respectable governments responsible for how the country money is distributed and for what purposes.

He applied to be a photographed and video recorded representative for universal dentist.

And applied earlier than anyone to be the same type of representative for the COVID-19 vaccines great success's in saving lives planet-wide. He called it my piece of the active plan.

INVADERS FROM EARTH

Are we more advanced then they? Why? Why what? Why did they all of a sudden want to leave? What do you mean by that? What happened after those hundreds of thousands of years living there that they desired to seek a different home? Did you not read where their atmosphere was so cold? I ask you the same question about us earthlings why do we want to escape out climate? Hunh do you mean to say that you are comfortable with volcanos, earthquakes, tornados, tsunamis and such? And if what I just asked is not enough, how do you

Are we more advanced than they?

Feel constantly living under the threat we see in so many movies just waiting for an extinguishing life event meteor to ice age us? O.K. new question why do they want to come here?

SEE WHOM I LIKE

Did you see the photo of Jane M. Hargatay and that luscious old guy looking each other with wet tounges on each others necks? She's one big star but that just puts it all out there doesn't it?

That super lucky sot just a year ago hit that four billion dollar lottery. He got almost three and a quarter bil for his share after taxes. Immediately he gets his set changed. Went from tiny spy. Glass penis to a fat fourteen inch fatty.

And applied earlier than anyone else to be the same type of representative for the COVID-19 vaccines great success's in saving lives planet-wide. He called it my piece of the active plan.

Bade all over the world have been trying to hook him. You can bet in a few months whose bootay is gonna get huge. Suppose she's not the kind to take it up there? Her lunch partner inquired two and three quarter billion dollars companied with multiple massive orgasms!

Thinking the lunch partner adds on. You know if that is true. Add to that big bottom thong lips protruding like Ludwig van Drake.

THE LEAD IN

Aaaaachoo, aaachooo, ahaachooo. Loud as he pleased. Being in his own bedroom and alone comfortability needn't even bother negate him from covering his nose. Neither was his oral cavity opening overcame.

Leonard Nomoy's, Zeachery Quinto and Chris Pine again snatched away the attentiveness carting a needed assemblage. The thoughts gathered had been accomplished over two years and the execution of ever shorter stories third addition had drawn high but now possessed transcended to its present ambigvity onto the movie. Both spocks!! Okay so he is guilty. Ink was to pour from this implement but confliction also exist. He felt like a danged twix candy bar. Should a beautiful, sexy, naked female by his willing to put her feet up and as far as pass taking a lead off, then he wouls he certain of apprehension and the title of the great songstess cher's record would not be happing. However just in an event where god decided to reel in his exhuberent confidence, where the tartorus is thee acetylsalicylic acid?

BROOKLYN'S

Marsha, Eliza, Brithelle and Bolive all six and seven years old girls from the block were playing games on the side walk. Deadman, their favorite they got from the boys not allowing the girls to play dead man on the asphalt markings in the street. Hop scotch and some game they had made up.

There was supposed to be no reason the parents needed to watch for their safety. This block was known throughout this quadrant as being under Luigi Giuseppi;s protection. This block Lousa Eloisa Giuseppi his niece abode. Marsha one of the three girls was legs's best friend. Louisa was called legs be marsha a first due to Lousia three initials that made up her whole names acciass the street sat Shetzar, Luigi's neighborhood arms dealer. His three year old Chevrolet impala was parked in front of the stoop She tear sat up on. He posture was always perfect. An example for the reminding the little juice, the girls to maintain poise when doing ever thing except for when at play. He would not smoke near them. He only drink when the squirts were around milk, juice or ice cream sodas. Never soda unfancied.

Today Patsy came on the block. Patsy was Britelle's older sister Patsy came over from school every now and then. Everybody loved Patsy except for Joe Robbi up the street but the two were decent friends. Patsy had five years ago beat out Joe by point two percent as valediction at Franoesco franco high school. Both were in there classes top two percentile at there respective post graduation university's Joe robbi came home only for Christmas and family reunion's.

Bringing up Joe Robbi at the vey self same moment Though three hours earlier in time zone Joe finds himself in school class law litigation his role is judge. Both parties have concluded their cases and court decision is about to be made by Robbin "Justice is blind and is supposed to be so. She is that way in order as there is to be legality between race, religion, sex and national origin. Today it has been given to me the commitment on the case before this classroom. I must in all fairness to my classroom peers inform that had I been on the side I must legally rule against than the losing side today would have been victorious" having to clear his threat slightly to restore acreditable order to his classes more forum. He continues on "The way the case was presented by the loser is a mockery. And by legal standards I must make a mockery. And by legal standards I must make a mockery of what I knew in my heart and what I know in my mind ought to be my decision.

Just has been blinded on this day but not for the righteousness she was blindfolded for. In my own words I say this and with enough effect as to give you all my full connotation. "he exhales exasperated as he lowers his head. His chin lands on clavicle. He says head held there." today, justice has been fucked.

Today, not only has Justice been fucked but justice has been fucked in the ass. I most due to legality find in opposition to plaintiff only" he emphasise as he fully faces his classmates and his academic sombre faced and eyes dispirited. Because plaintiff's representation was at its very best totally inadequate"

Professor Messeau next called the case arguing could it be feasible for the United States to be obliterated using the claim of a massive contageon outbreak in the US with an outlook of world wide contamination ending all human life!

ONE STEP BEYOND

Two bored doctors were in a titty bar before the show started. Do you want to hear a joke? Asked the older of the two. Yes. Yeah why not. It's kind of racist if you push it. How come a yellow haired woman is a blonde? How come a brown haired women is a brunette yet a red head and a bald woman is a bald head? The younger physician contemplates and concedes. I do not know. Neither do I say the elder of the two but once you pass the white head's nomenclature you'd better shot up before you name the black haired one.

Yours Truly, Rodney

The whole world ended yesterday. The entire world is gone. There remains nothing. No. That's not true. Even nothing is gone. Yes nothing ended yesterday the same as something. There is no one left so you don't even have a brain to figure that out. Yeah. Your brain ended yesterday too. Go ahead ask yourself how can. I be here to write this. The only real question that would have mattered is why am I writing this. No one will be around to real it I ended. I am not dead. Dead ended yesterday. To make it easy tomorrow is not coming. When tomorrow comes it won't be tomorrow because it ended yesterday. I think that time I finally got to meat Cher. Good piece of ass. Good hell! Great piece of ass. Truth is it never happened but nobody's gonna say anything about that lie. Yesterday everything ended. Today is all there is. Your play no need to be hung like a horse as of tomorrow because everything ended..... Yesterday.

ABOUT THE AUTHOR

Mr. Rodney Paul Williams the six child born of Leona Demaris Banks was given the name Rodney Paul Wallace of birth. He was born in year of nineteen fifty three.

At the age of nine years old in Philadelphia, Pennsylvania in the country of the United States of America he made a request of his mother to change his last name from Rodney Paul Wallace. She gave him his request, thus the name Williams became his legal sir name.

When graduation high school with honours, he turned down all of his college scholarships. He realized later in the life that. That was a huge turn of events, into the wrong direction.

It disappointed a hard working mother.

After being honorably discharged from the air force, part of the USA's armed forces he finally attended CCP where he wrote the first of over two hundred short stories in a four part series titled even shorter stories.

He is now working on a full length novel

Still he in today's time wishes to achieve a dream of making a video in the snows of South Africa.